THE CITY
MELVILLE BRIDGE
SHNARN TOWERS
SUNSHINE'S TOP HAT
ORSON'S AIRSHIP
DR. WYETH'S LAIR
WILD DOGS
MEAN CHILD JUNKYARD
ANGEL CLIFFS
RACHEL FOREST
MERMAID ROCKS
DOLL FACTORY
THE DOLL FACTORY
PERCY'S LIGHTHOUSE
CASTLE POND
KARAMOZOV CASTLE
N.B.N.G. CEMETARY
FLAGG BEACH

Pop Gun War : Gift

by Farel Dalrymple

dedicated to my mother

Introduction

Dowsing for story

Pop Gun War marks the unassuming debut of an auspicious new talent. Farel Dalrymple walks a dreaming urban ledge, feeling the spit and grit and cobblestones of the city through his soles, while his eyes glance upward, giving us glimpses of poesy and magic. It is this tension, between naturalist narrative and fantastic possibility, that so disarms the reader of Pop Gun War.

Dalrymple arrives on the heels of a terrific legacy of artists; charmed souls who knew how to let the unconscious feed the conscious, and in doing so, found gold. The tradition is rich-painters like Odilon Redon, Salvador Dalí, and Paul Klee; filmmakers such as Luis Buñuel and Jean Cocteau; writers the likes of Jack Kerouac and Gabriel García Márquez; and the masters of parable that created The Wizard of Oz and Alice In Wonderland. These artists, like Dalrymple, seem to have access to the hypnagogic state: that sexy, syrupy nether realm between dream and awake, rich in floating symbols. That place Carl Jung called "the collective unconscious," collective in that the symbols don't feel meaningless and random, they feel universal. It's not unlike dowsing for water; a man holds a forked stick. He grips it, unsure. Will it dip over water? How does that work? Perhaps by letting the unconscious take over, letting things flow through that would otherwise be blocked. Deeper truths. Universal meaning. Water under dirt. But to find the water you seek, your hands must be true and steady. From the very first pages of Pop Gun War #1, when a tough angel pays to have his wings chain-sawed off, a little boy retrieves them from the garbage, and with a glance over shoulder to see emerging wing stubs, one senses in Dalrymple a sure-footed, lyrical storyteller.

Dalrymple's narrative linguistics are all his own: the choreography is natural one moment, the next a lurch into dream, yet somehow still holding logic, as the lurch was based in something true to the story – a scheme, an ill intent, an unfettered desire. Who wouldn't want to grow wings and fly? Everyone has flying dreams, so isn't this as real a narrative element as the walls and floors of a story? Hitchcock once said that all films are "chase dreams," and the description fits Pop Gun War. Dalrymple crafts the meander of city life, then punctuates it with narrative ellipses–with a cinematic run through streets, into the warp of dream, lines like: "I have a lucky footprint. It gets stepped in every day," and the pause of perfectly placed pin-up as the story catches its breath. Infused with humor (a short man tells a short story on a short walk), the stories are intimate without being sentimental, and have not so much villains so as toxic people that infect others with ill will, only to be deflected by the good will of "heroes" of the tale.

Graced with simple, stark covers, sometimes revealing the tender, slack body language of children (resigned yet wise, ready for anything), this is a wonderful collection. As one reads, there is ever a delicate suspicion, a holy notion, that each story is actually populated by characters from dream, searching for the one who dreamt them.

Ann Nocenti
New York City
3/03

PROLOGUE
Hey, It's mine.
HAW HAW.
Clang clang
Crunch
I raise!
SLAP!

clang
clang
clang

Welcome home.

Yes, It is a bit cluttered I know.
Now that we're together I no longer need these things.
I will make this right.

Come Children. Receive your last toys.
I no longer need them.

It feels good...
eh?

Hisssssss

uh...

heh heh.

Snap!

MR. GRIMSHAW
SINCLAIR
EMILY
RACHEL
ROGER
THE RICH KID
PERCY
ADDISON
SUNSHINE MONTANA

chapter one- lucky footprint

CRASH!

READING
HOSIERY
UNDERWEAR
22
BZZZZT
BZZZZZZZZZZZ

BZZ ZBZZZ ZZZ
ZZZZT
FWOOSH

HELP
RIDGE SUPER MARKET
SLAM!

Smith's
Smith's
BAR-CAFE
NO STANDING
MUSIC

Hi, everyone. We're the Emilies.
one... two... three... four

Schaefer

Sinclair?
Hi, Rachel.
Why aren't you inside watching your sister play?

I'm not old enough...
Besides... I've seen her play before.

I had a dream last night about my mother

I was at her wedding to my father.
My sister was there. Everyone was there.
Dance with me, Sinclair.
It didn't matter that I hadn't been born yet.
The memory was real.
and very dear to me.

SIC
wake up, weirdo.
hey, stupid...
...Look out.
BONK
HA HA HA HA
you stupid bum! you stink!
HA! HA!
Yeah, you ugly old man...
Take a shower!
Spit!
SPLAT!
HA HA HA HA

HEY!

Leave that man alone.

huh?

Boy...

...Where did you get those wings?

get him.

Oh no, Mr. Addison, you lay back down.

I said...
no.

KRACK!

I've slept enough.

SMACK

oh.

HEY!

Wha..? wha..? pant pant

Ohmygod. pant What did you do?

huh?
whoa.

This place stinks.
Yeah, let's get out of here.
Forget about that boy. Listen to me now...
Music?
HEY!
Hey! Old man! Slow down.
You're getting tired from this long walk.
Just sit down for a minute.
Take a rest.

Smith's BAR
NO! Don't go in here.
Get a drink, but don't do it here.

...I'm not allowed in there.

♫I have a lucky footprint.♪

♪It gets stepped in everyday.♫

Come have a seat, friend.

You have to come out sometime, you filthy bum!
MUSIC

CURTAINS
WALL
FLOOR
RUG
WHUMP!
CHAIR2

ok. a new label.
OK. there.
BOY W/ WINGS
Everything gets a label
Why?
Because people don't always know what things are.
SHIRT

Oh.
Hey, Even all your pets have labels.
yes.
CAT 4

You sure have a lot of cats.

Yes, they are faithful friends. Unconditional love.
PANTS

Why are you crying?
I don't know.

I think that I'm afraid.

You can keep your label.
CEILING
BOY W/ WINGS
WALL
CURTAIN 4

I'm never getting old.
Soul man's on the run...

Making jokes and having fun...
Lie here awhile with me...
licks some wounds, feel glee...
tap
tap
Times in the head...
Butt's in the bed...

Pull those covers high
USIC
Someday you'll die

Just hunker down
Be the clown

You've still got time

It's in your mind.

NEXT
a dwarf,
a monk,
and a fish.

Sinclair
Emily
Addison
KOOLE
THE RICH KID
Percy
Rachel
SUNSHINE
ROGER

chapter two- translation

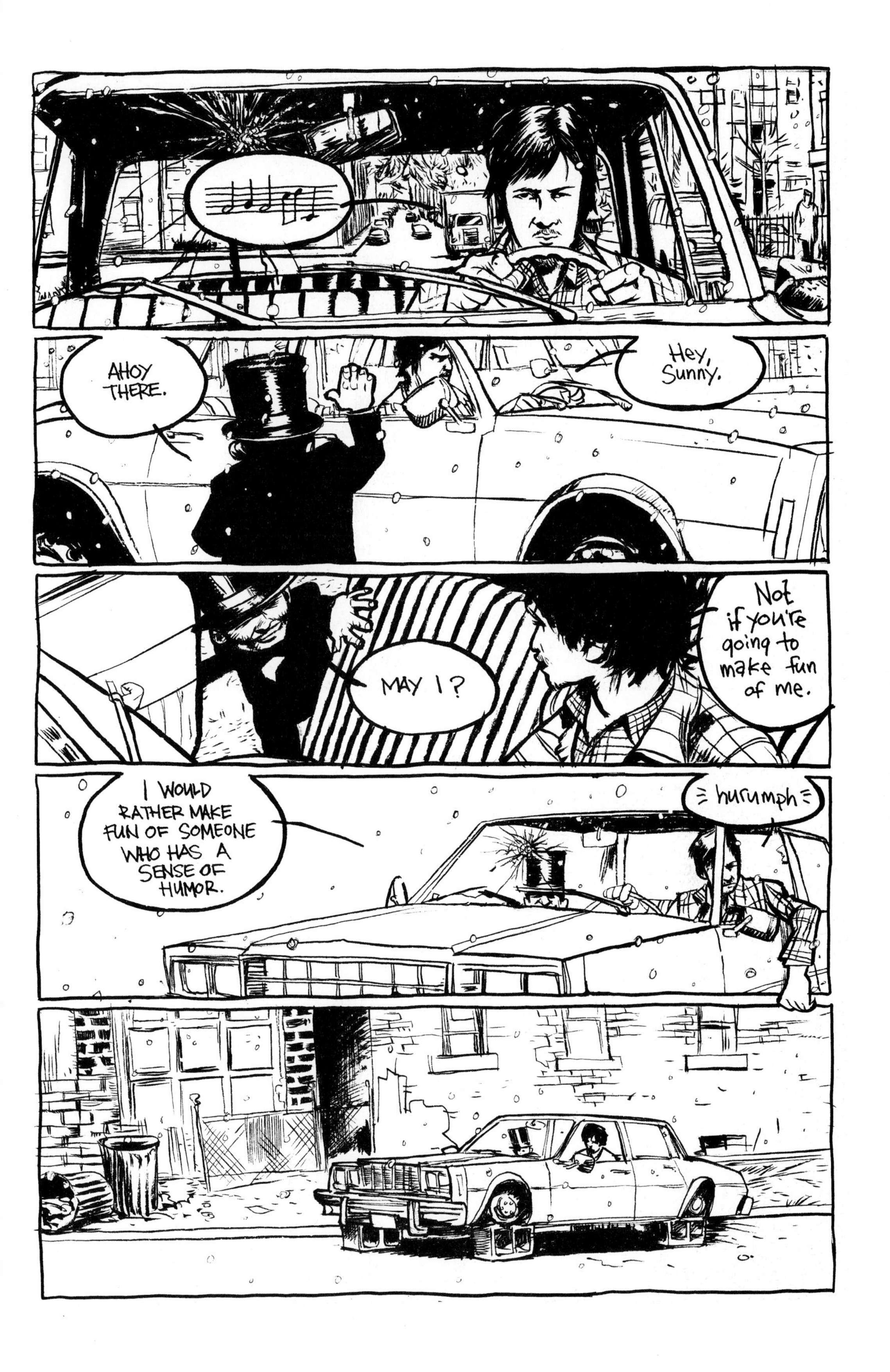
AHOY THERE.
Hey, Sunny.
MAY I?
Not if you're going to make fun of me.
I WOULD RATHER MAKE FUN OF SOMEONE WHO HAS A SENSE OF HUMOR.
≡ hurumph ≡

Well, would you look at this guy?
YES, IT'S "KOOLE"
THIS MONK'S NOT HERE TO BLESS US EH?
IS HE ONE OF YOUR PROJECTS?
nah.
He has a whole bunch of guys working him over.
HEY!
Hey, Crazy!
clang clang
clang clang
Come over here!
aww, nobody listens to me anymore.
clang clang clang
HE CERTAINLY IS CREEPY LOOKING.
yeah. heh..heh...

...What a creep.
Hisssss
HAHAHA
HAHAHAH
HA HA
hee hee
clang
clang

Hello, sir.
Cold day out, eh?
Not to me.
But I dont argue with bums.
There's no point in it.
What?
Sounds like my cue.
This might be fun.
WELL, I HAVE SOME THINGS TO TAKE CARE OF TOO.
BE SEEING YOU.
Hey, Addison,
Who's your friend?
ummm.
I'm not his friend

Thanks for watching our stuff.
sure.
Are you coming to the show tonight?
Of course.
Great. see you there.
IPDX-455
Addison.
Hey, Sinclair.
Was that my sister leaving...?
Hey! Why are you here?!
huh?
Leave Addison alone.

Those don't belong to you, boy.
Did you steal them?
They're mine.
I found them.
Sinclair, Who are you talking to?
This weirdo over here?
You stole those wings!!
Hey now!
no.
clang clang
They were a gift.
thief!
Liar!
thief!
clang clang
They were a gift.

clang clang
clang
clang
clang
clang
clang
clang
clang
clang

a hem
Sunny, How are you?
GOOD DAY MA'AM.
I SEEM TO HAVE LOST MY FISH.
I THOUGHT HE MIGHT BE AROUND HERE SOMEWHERE.
today I heard a fish crying from a basement apartment.
I tried to talk to him but he wouldn't speak.
I can take you there if you like
— SPLENDID!
ON THE WAY I WILL TELL YOU A STORY
It's not that far.
OH, IT IS A SHORT STORY.

CA
BOUNCE!
OK Lewis, yer out.
Hey! it's the cops!
oh, man.
Run!
Hey, wait.
1360
Hey!

Why were you running?
Shut up, Sinclair! you don't know anything!
We weren't doing anything wrong.
yeah.
I saw a lady calling the cops.
nah, you guys are stupid.
those cops just drove away.
Why would they be after us?
Sinclair, you think you're so smart.
leave us alone.

Broc, wait up.
Broc...?
Hey, man...
Gee, Sinclair,
We were having fun.
Why did you have to ruin it?

He's down there.
YAY FOR ME. KOOLE IS GOING OUT THIS EVENING.
MANY THANKS, MY LADY.
SUNSHINE MONTANA IS FLYING SOLO FROM HERE.
Clang
Clang
Clang
SUCCESS
JUST LOOK AHEAD
GIVE YOUR BEST
KEEP ON TRYING
TAKE THE TEST
!
PIC
PIC
PIC
PIC
Percy?
There you are.

IT TOOK A WHILE THIS TIME.
BUT AT LAST I FOUND YOU.
WE'LL ALWAYS FIND EACH OTHER.
ROGER HUMAN
PLAYING ON JAN 6, 10:00
TONIGHT 9:00 THE EMILIES
$5 COVER
JAN 19
no bodies no graves
clang clang clang
Oh great.
clang clang clang
Emily, It's the president of our fan club.
Just be cool, Jay.

Koole?
clang
that's my name.
clang clang
uhhh.
whoah.
hee hee.
No!
yep.
Who?
ALL AGES
RHB
THE RAPTURE
MONA GRITCH
THE
EMILIES
TONIGHT
9:00

AGES SHOW
R.H.B. 8:00
PILOT TO GUNNER 9:00
THE RAPTURE 10:00
THIS WEDNESDAY
Ding
Hey, chill out, buddy.
You!
The thief!
You took my fish!
What!
clang clang
Give him back!
You're crazy, man!
clang clang

Hey! hold on, pal.
Clang
Clang
Just relax, ok?
?!
What do you have on under those those robes?
touchy hands...
Don't touch me with those touchy hands!
ooooffff!
claang
I'll show you.
clang
clang
clang
clang
...Show you how it feels!
clang
clang

PUNCH!
clang
clang
Why?
I was better than all of you
Riiiipp!
nothing
I have nothing now
I used to be special.
special

Sinclair, are you ok? ...
...oh
I'm Sorry, Sinclair
"O, what a panic's in thy breastie!"
Hey, Sinclair.
Hi, Emily.
Are you... coming home for dinner?

no, I don't think so.
oh.
Addison?
yeah?
Those wings really were a gift.
I know, Sinclair.
No,
really... look.

Well, I'll be...
Wow.
You know, Sinclair.
Everything turned out ok.
You're pretty lucky.
THIS IS GREAT.

OUT HERE BY THIS CLIFF.
SITTING IN THIS FURNITURE.
YOU'RE NEXT TO ME.
IT'S JUST HOW IT SHOULD BE.
I USED TO WORK IN A GROCERY STORE.
I AM JUST SO WEARY OF LISTENING TO OTHER PEOPLE'S INEPT CONVERSATIONS.
NOW LOOK AT US.

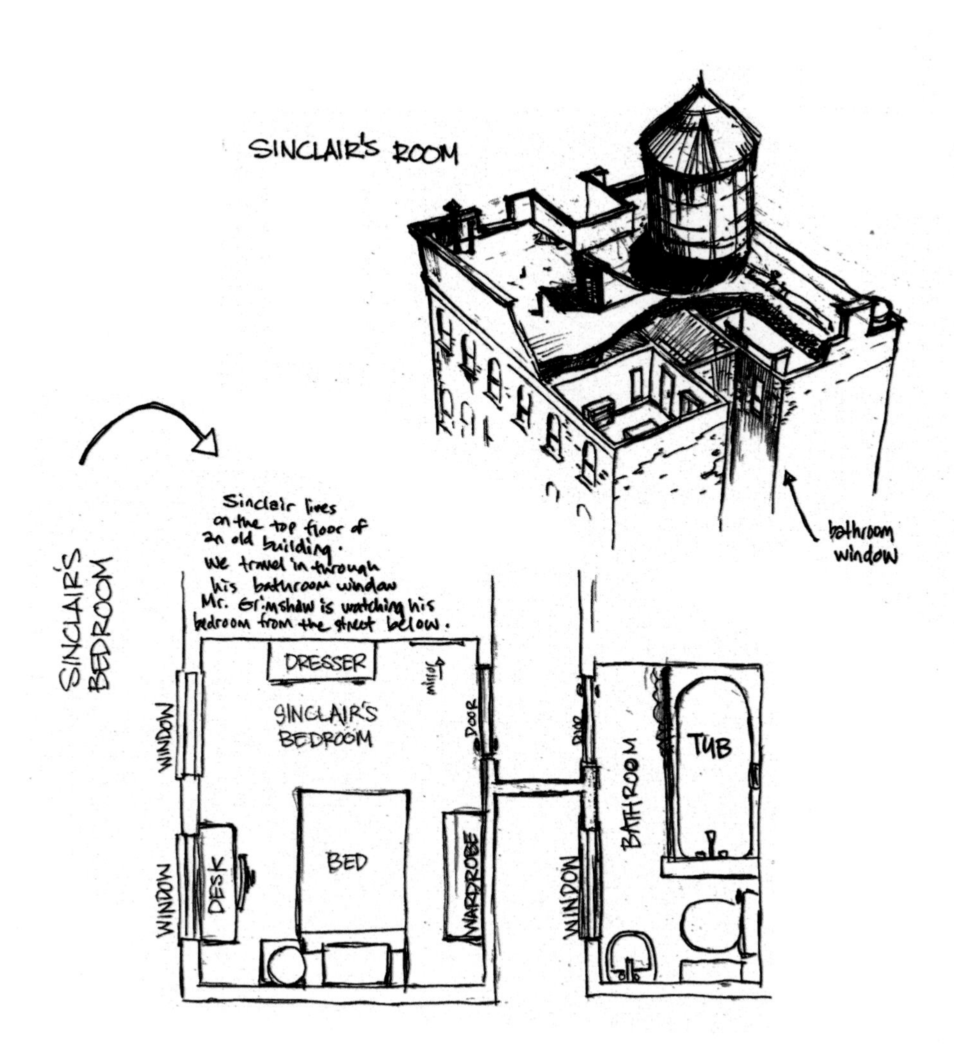
SINCLAIR'S ROOM
bathroom window
SINCLAIR'S BEDROOM
Sinclair lives on the top floor of an old building. We travel in through his bathroom window Mr. Grimshaw is watching his bedroom from the street below.
DRESSER
mirror
SINCLAIR'S BEDROOM
DOOR
WINDOW
WINDOW
DESK
BED
WARDROBE
DOOR
BATHROOM
TUB
WINDOW

chapter three - the living insult

So what is it like being a child genius?
I mean, being so young, you...
uhhh...
yeah, well... I agreed to do this interview...
Look, can't we talk about something other than my age?
Sure, sure, of course. ummm...
Did you always know that you were different than the other children you knew?
Isn't everybody different?
A lot of my songs are about that,
being in this city...
... with all of the weirdness around us...
Sure, sure. That's great.
So, your critics say you are too young, that you are hiding your immaturity behind cryptic lyrics.
Some people resent you for your age.

WOW.

What a complete waste of time.
TONIGHT A
SMITHS
THE EMILIES
ANCIENT JUSTIC
ROGER HUMAN BE

WHA!

Watch it, Jerk!

Why don't people pay attention?
grumble grumble

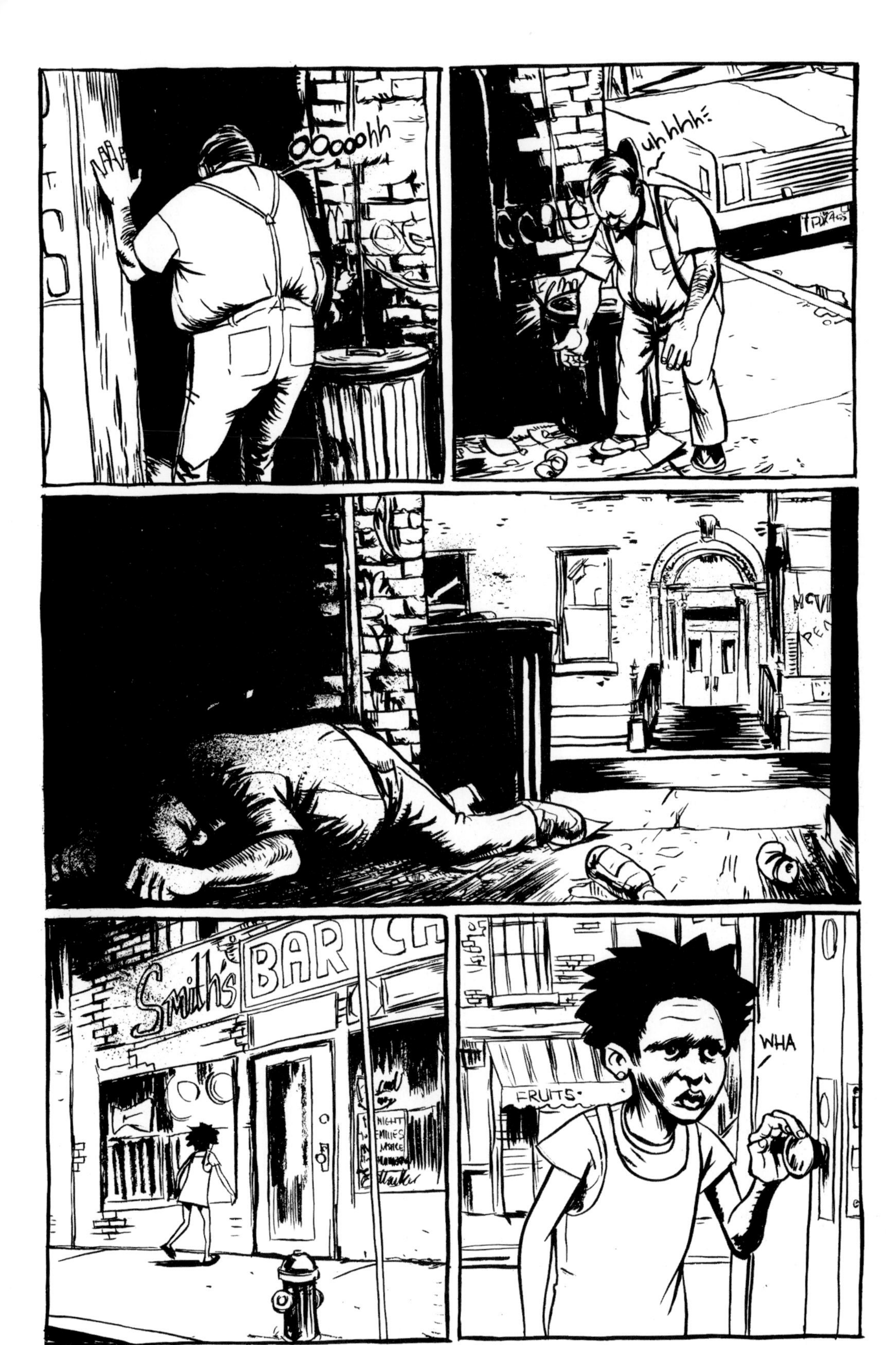
OOooohh
uhhhh
Smith's BAR
FRUITS
WHA

What is he doing here?
He said he knew you.

Look, that stupid interveiw is over.
Sure, Sure.
My apologies for the ruse, Ms. Emily.
I am not a journalist at all but actually a representative for a magnificent corporation.
We are offering you an exclusive contract with us.
We can give you the money and exposure you need to become the next rock sensation.
gee mister, that's great!
How did you know that's exactly what we wanted.

I'm sure you're really good at making money,
but we're a band, not a sensation.
sell this to someone else, thanks.
CONTRACT
yeah, we're awesome dudes who like to rock.
heh heh heh
ok.
Make 'em sign.
Huh, that's it? No more sales pitch?
No,
You will sell yourselves to someone,
Probably in such small ways you might not realize it is happening.
It's your loss for not cashing in now.

SPACE FOR RENT
SHOE REPAIR
SHOE
SMITHS
BAR-CAFE
26
ANTIQUES
TRADING

Hey, brother, mind if I take a sit next to you?
Zzzz
This is brilliant. An artist like you deserves a gallery
Wealth and fame are now yours.
Nice leather Jacket, dummy.
I've been making art since I got eighteen.
But is it worthwhile? what's the point, right?
yeah... I don't know...

...I Just have to make it
Shave it!
Wow. You should've kept it.
ugly suit fatso.
R.K., you are getting so small I can barely hear you.
You can't make me feel bad anymore.
yeah, you're just getting so fat you're listening to some other jerk now.

...Now that you are appearing in films and doing photo shoots...
...What is your response to critics who say you have lost your edge?
I'm happy. There are more important things to me now than being cutting edge.
...Things like being a good father, husband, and providing for my family.
scratch scratch
you're no fun anymore.
Z

blub blub
blub
blub blub
stay up!
Stupid boat.

Who am I? Who are you?
Weird, have I lived my whole life as this person?
WHOAH! I almost went crazy there.
Hey, who's that?
scratch scratch

What a weirdo.
HAH HA. It's a clip-on.
mmm... Just a few more minutes' sleep.
honk honk
Huh?
How long was I asleep?
Oh. Just a minute.
honk
honk
honk

honk honk
honk
HEY, QUIT HONKING, DUMMY!
Why are you honking anyway?
honk
SHUT UP!
SHUT UP!
SHUT UP!
SHUT THAT STUPID CAR HORN UP!
hmm...
What a jerk that guy is for yelling like that

Jerk.

LISTEN, CHILDREN. LISTEN CAREFULLY.
WE MUST FIGHT.
FIGHT ALL OF THE ENEMIES OF OUR INTELLIGENCE.
YOUR THOUGHTS CAN CREATE BEASTS IN YOU.
DEFEAT YOUR ADVERSARIES BY THINKING THROUGH THEM.
I USED TO WORK IN A GROCERY STORE.
NOW WATCH.
I AM GROWING.

YOUR INTEREST MADE ME GROW.
Sunshine.
Be careful, Sunshine.
RACHEL, I HAVE IT ALL IN HAND.
your children are leaving.
WHAT?
HEY!
ABE'S GROCERY
RESTURANT
WAIT!
WHERE ARE YOU GOING?

Gentlemen, really listen to what your heart is saying.
Give her your time.
Try to be rock and roll,
throw trash on the ground.
you will look cool.
Walk slow. Act tough.
Dont think too much.
Maybe even smoke a cigarette.
follow me.
WHAT ABOUT ME?
You were fun to watch when you were little, but now...
...He's got a head in a bag. That's neat.

HEY, ROCK AND ROLL!
WHY CAN'T YOU BE LIKE ME AND PUT YOUR TRASH IN THE TRASH CAN?

YOU DUMP ON MY CITY!
I'LL DUMP ON YOU.
I'LL DUMP ON YOU.
YOU TOO, PERCY?
I'M NOT COOL ENOUGH ANYMORE, EH?
GO ON THEN.
I'LL KEEP GROWING.

HANUKA
SERVICES
127 WEST 26 ST
AUTO REPAIRS
155
E 26 ST
STAR WIND TRAVEL

TIME TO GO.

C'MON, BE A DANDY.

I JUST HAD THE STRANGEST DREAM.

IT'S PROBABLY NOT AS STRANGE AS THE ONE I'M HAVING.

Chapter 4 - Sinclair and Addison

emily?

Where are you?

#$@!!
CRASH!
*%#$@
$@#☆?
155E
PIZZA
SMASH!
%☆$!!!
IPX-455
@*!!

155E
55E
@☆$!!

disgusting

mmmm.

GREAT FOODS
BEANS
yeah.

RITE
DELI & GROCERY
159
SPECIAL 2.99!

chips
mmm...
HEY!
?
AHA!
YOU STEAL MY STUFF? GEDDOUDA MY STORE!
but... I didn't..

These are my beans!
DEL
trip!

ooofff.
HA! HA!
Oh no!
Darn it!
Addison.
Hey, Sinclair.
Hey, have you seen Emily anywhere?
Nope.
I haven't seen her for like a week.

I've already checked Smith's bar,
Melville Bridge,
the KRP building,
Bogo tower,
Schnarn Towers,
and Gilpin Park.
hmmm... let's go ask Sunshine Montana.
...but first let's get some food.
*6!!
My breakfast plans got ruined.
*$%@
Hey. You two! Geddouda here with those!
$*#!!!

%@#!
SMASH!
CRASH!
*%$@
#@ϟ!!!
Rachel said she saw Sunshine over...
Hey, Sunshine.
WOW.

HELLO, GENTLEMEN.
"Not by beef or by bread are giants made or nourished."

AH YES, "AND THE GIANT'S FACE ON THE DWARF'S SHOULDERS IS FRIGHTENED."
Sunshine, have you seen my sister anywhere?

I FEAR THAT I HAVE NOT, YOUNG MASTER.
YOU MAY BE INTERESTED TO CHECK WITH MY FRIEND BEN ABLE.
HE IS A PRIVATE INVESTI-GATOR.
SUITS
555-3786

Okay, Sunshine, Thanks... Don't get too big.
"TOO BIG FOR MY BRITCHES?" I CERTAINLY HAVE NEVER HEARD THAT BEFORE.

All right, children,
are you ready to listen?
YYYAAAAAAAAAYYY!!
Ok, now be attentive!

**$!!!
@#%!

What's this?

WHACK!
uhhg!

uuuhn.... STOP! I work for a large corporation !!!
Run children! Run!

WHUP!
WHUD!
Ooooffff! run! uuuhngh!

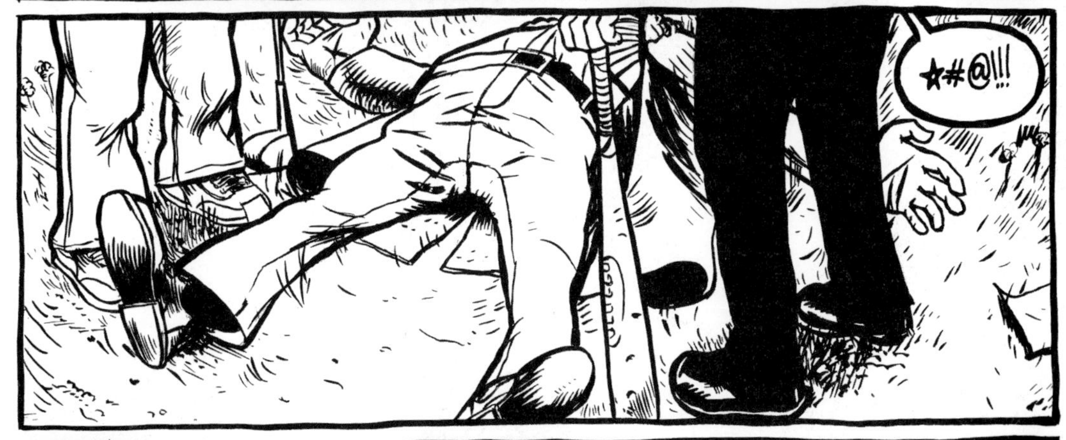
*#@!!!

?

knock knock
yes, come in.
hello.
yes, sit down.
I'm looking for my sister.
Sunshine said you could help.
Y-Yes, I'm good at helping people.
first, I only work alone.
scribble scribble
Yes, now shall we discuss payment?
I'll need some money upfront.

Uhhh, Addison, I don't think...
yes...
I'm blind!
HELP ME!
yaaa! let go!
Sinclair!

Sinclair?
Why did you run?
I don't know.
I was scared.
Why did you?
I wasn't running!
I was just coming out here to see what you were doing!
oh.
I think I'm gonna go home now. I'm tired and stuff.
ok.

I'll keep asking about Emily.
★◎$!!!
*&#?
$★%!!!
SMASH

*%☆!!!
@$#⚡
☆%$!!!
HUH?
crunch.

creak
Who's there?

Emily
Hey Sinclair.

I'm gonna crash here tonight.
I'm exhausted.

ok.
I Just got back from a short tour with RHB and Ancient Justice.

That sounds like fun.
yeah...
What did you do today?

oh, nothing.
z...

z...

good night.

NO PARKING
groan
unh. run children.

I work for a great corporation.

Wait, you fool! Don't leave me.
Who are you?
Give me back to Mr. Grimshaw!
?
Give me back. You Jerk!

Can I have some extra for our friend?
C'mon, not during dinner, dog.
...
lick lick

Act tough and throw your trash on the ground.

chapter five - bicycle messenger

1 Soul's Midnight
Doll
FAC

Doll.
FACTORY
WHO?
WHO DID THIS?!
gulp
ONE OF MY FINEST CREATIONS, THE DISEMBODIED HEAD, IS LOST.
THIS CITY WILL TREMBLE.
Don't worry, sir.
...Tremble.
I believe the children got away safely.

THE CHILDREN? ...

YES,... GATHER THEM....

...LULL THEM HERE...

COME SEE
SOUL'S MIDNIGHT
a new production
of puppets and fun
THE DOLL FACTORY
presented by
KING DOLL

... WITH PROMISES OF ENTERTAINMENT.

Doll.
FACTORY
PIZZA
FOR LADIE
WE WILL KEEP THEM HERE WITH US.

2
Lonely City

Dear Emily,
I hope your tour with Soophie Nun Squad and the Bright Lights is going well. Mom and I miss you a real lot. The city seems even more deserted than usual today. Yesterday I had a bad bicycle accident.
I skinned both my knees and tore my pants. I am glad no one saw me fall. Right before I fell I had a really great idea about something. After the fall I couldn't remember what it was. I still can't remember. What if that idea could have changed my life?
maybe it would have made us rich.
Now I will never know.
Love,
your brother,
Sinclair. xxo
clack
kick

CITY PAPER
WHERE ARE OUR CHILDREN?
HUNDREDS VANISH OVERNIGHT
MAYOR STUMPED.
Smith's
Rachel.

Hello, Sinclair. I'm glad you didn't go with all of those other children.
You know where they are?

huh?
I bet he knows.

me?
grumble

Go ask Percy.
He saw the children following Mr. Grimshaw somewhere.
awww...
ring

That Mr. Grimshaw is a big phoney.
He's full of crud.

ring ring
I'd rather just ride my bike around.

Hah!
You're Jealous you didn't get invited.

SHUT UP!
Why are you here?
You're always messing with Addison.

Sinclair, Addison went with the children.

Really?

Yeah, you should go find your friend.
Do you hear the voices too?

You're just mad 'cause now you don't have anyone to hassle.

I'm bothering you, aren't I?

3 Articulation

WHACK! WHACK!
clap clap HAHAHAHA clap clap YAAYY! clap clap clap clap clap clap woohoo
THE END.
DID YOU LOVE IT, CHILDREN?
It was really cool but can we go home now?
Yeah, I'm tired.
I miss my mom.
Yeah, we wanna go.
no.

yeah, king doll, let 'em go.
HEY!..
YOU WEREN'T INVITED!
HOW DID YOU GET IN?
percy showed me.
TAKE PERCY AND GET!

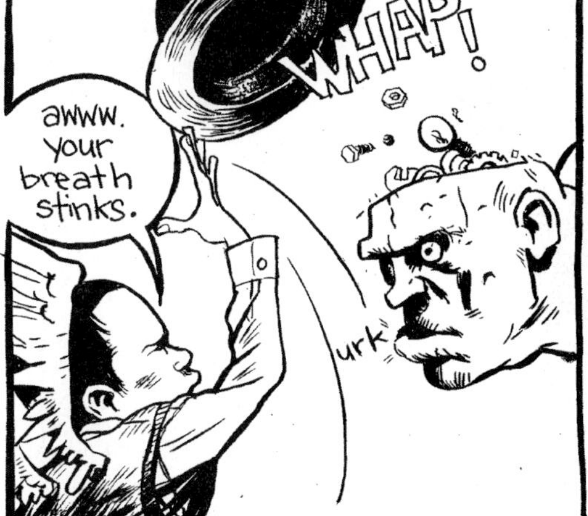
WHAP!
awww. your breath stinks.
urk

you're not scary.
you play with dolls.

I read The Wizard of OZ.
RRIIIIIPP
I know how this stuff works.
no.
You are all my puppets.
Hey, you can't keep these children here.
but it's not fair.
It's a violent city they live in.
Mr. Grimshaw was beaten. It took me days to repair him.

I lost one of my greatest puppets, "The head in the bag."
These children should not be left to run around this violent city.
I need to control such things.
awww, go on and make your dumb puppets,
but you're crazy if you think you can control everything.

WHY NOT?!!
uh oh
WHO IS MORE POWERFUL THAN ME, HAROLD DOLLPIMPLE,
KING DOLL!
you may have exposed me but I still have my creations.
grab!
grip!

CRUUUUNCH!
wha...
PERCY?

THERE YOU ARE.
GULP.
Ahh, Supernatural intervention.
Hey! When did you get here?
I've been here the whole time.
I've been here the whole time, Sinclair.

oh, GOOD DAY, GENTELMEN.

NOW THAT MY COMPATRIOT AND I ARE REUNITED WE WILL BE ON OUR WAY.

BACK TO THE SEA.

weird.
Just wait.

Bonk!
AHHR! You hit me in the ear!
Why the ear?!

I guess all of the kids are alright.

no one's hurt are they?

Hey!
That's my bike!
Hey, get off!
Why do you ride when you can fly?
sometimes it's more fun to ride.
you took some things of mine.

Not these!
These are my own!
Besides, you threw yours in a garbage can.
Yes. being normal sometimes requires giving up a gift.
I'll find my way back now.
I'm taking your bike.

Sinclair, Why do those kids always pick on me?

I don't know, Addison.

I guess some people just enjoy others' misery.

everyone's controlled by something.

Addison, you shouldn't let those kids pick on you.
I'd punch them.
I'm a good boxer.
Nah,
but I am going to start handling those situations better... start taking control of my life.
man, I miss my bike.
-ring
-ring

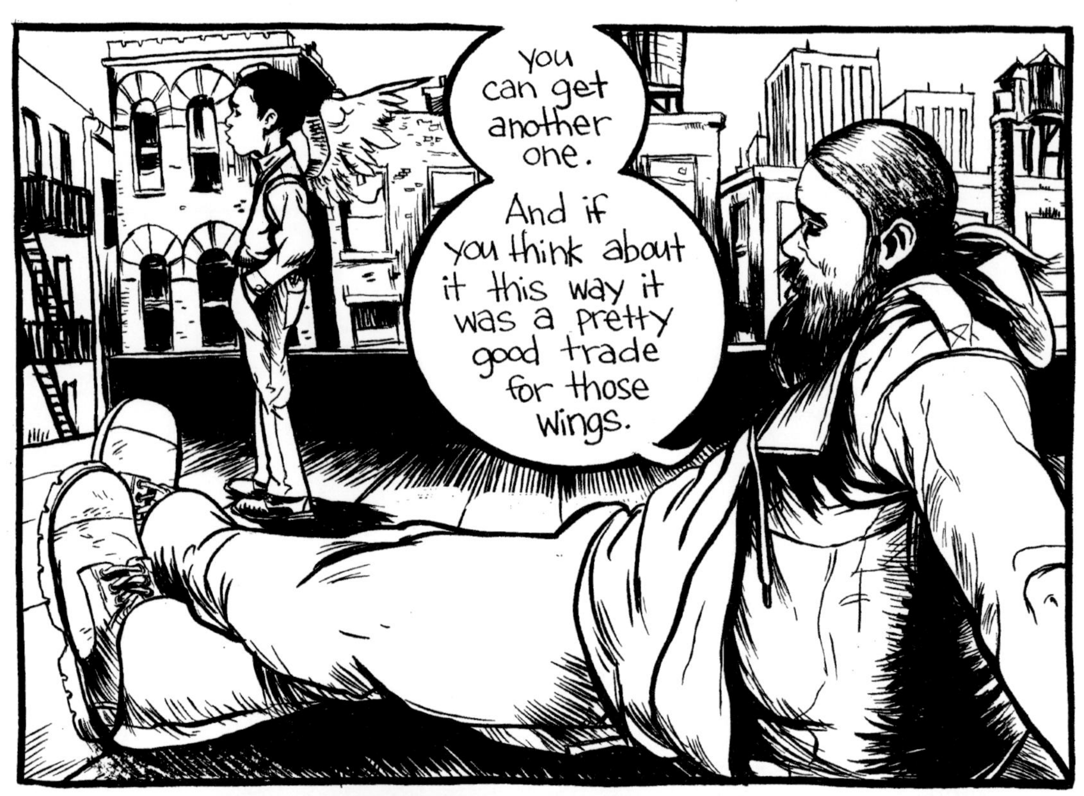
you can get another one.
And if you think about it this way it was a pretty good trade for those wings.

Yeah, I guess so.
except THESE wings have always been mine.

The end.

www.popgunwar.com

The contents of this book were created in New York City between 1999 and 2003

Emily's lyrics on pages 34 & 35 are from a poem by Sandra Dalrymple.
Addison's quote on page 95 is from Herman Melville's *Moby Dick.*
Sunshine's response on page 96 is from "Dwarf of Disintegration" by Oscar Williams.
The Rich Kid's quote on page 56 is from Robert Burns'
"To A Mouse, On Turning Her Up In Her Nest With The Plough."

special thanks to:
my family, Diana Schutz, Gillian Robespierre, Roger Human Being,
Bruce Waldman and Dominick Rapone in SVA the print shop,
Andy Boder and everyone from Alt.Coffee,
the Meathaus crew, and the Provance family,
S. Edward Irvin from Absence of Ink,

Some more special thanks to:
John Green and Dave Roman of Cryptic Press
Dan Zalkus, Peter Laird and the Xeric Foundation,
Paul Hornschemier, Bob Schreck, Tomer Hanuka,
the Society of Illustrators, Brandon Graham, Zac Baldus,
Serge Marcos, Jay Sacher, and the Keefe Family

and so many people over the years
who have helped me and told me they enjoyed this book

other books by Farel Dalrymple:
The Wrenchies
IT WILL ALL HURT
Delusional (the Graphic and sequential work of Farel Dalrymple)
Palefire (with author MK Reed)
Omega the Unknown (with author Jonathan Lethem)

pop gun war

"gift"

Original cover art for Dark Horse Comics edition, 2003

A.O.I.
SCRAP METALS

POP GUN WAR: GIFT

Published by Image Comics, Inc.
Office of publication: 2001 Center Street, Sixth Floor, Berkeley, CA 94704.

Contains previously published material collected from the original Pop Gun War comic book series and the Dark Horse Comics collection of the same name.

Printed in the USA. For information regarding the CPSIA on this printed material call: 203-595-3636 and provide reference #RICH-676542.
For international rights, contact: foreignlicensing@imagecomics.com.

ISBN: 978-1-63215-773-7

Diana Schutz original collection editor